ALEXANDER and the GREAT FOOD FIGHT

Written by Linda J. Hawkins
Illustrations by Jennifer D. Bowles

TURNER PUBLISHING COMPANY

Turner Publishing Company
412 Broadway • P.O. Box 3101
Paducah, Kentucky 42002-3101
(270) 443-0121

Library of Congress Control Number: 2002109062
ISBN: 1-56311-820-3

Turner Publishing Company Staff:
Amy Sietsma, Editor
Shelley R. Davidson, Designer

Printed in the United States of America.

Turner books are available at a special discount for
bulk purchases for fund-raising efforts, sales promotions
or educational use. Author and illustrator available for
speaking to children and book signings.
Call toll free 1-888-526-5589.

DEDICATION FROM THE AUTHOR

This book is dedicated to all the children who've brought me happiness as only a child can.

To my husband of twenty-nine years, for helping me raise two wonderful sons, Derek and Jeremy.

To our little bundle of joy, my first biological grandchild, Jenna Raylin.

To all the children who've shared a part of my life, I still say "Eat your good foods first, leaving space for only a small dessert!"

Everyone is an individual uniquely made by a loving creator. We make many choices daily, good and bad. Some choose the wrong foods while looking for a snack. You've heard the saying "Money can't buy health," also Proverbs 8:19 says "My fruit is better than gold." We can be assured stronger, healthier bodies by choosing healthy foods from each food group, including the fruits. May this book help you improve your food choices so that you can give your body all the needed nutrients.

Author would like to thank her typist Denise C.; the Butler County Library staff Sibyl G., Connie E., Mary G., Kendra M. for seeing that I received all needed resources or books; to Professor Chloé L. for reviewing; to Licensed Dieticians Teresa H., Dwan G.; Food Director Jane S. for reviewing nutritional facts. Thanks to Mary B., Greg G., Heather U. who pushed me beyond my comfort zone. They also wanted to see my writing in print. To Amy, my editor that kept me informed and on track.

DEDICATION FROM THE ILLUSTRATOR

Dedicated to Nancy C. who taught me, my Mom who always believed in me, and especially to Jacob and Jullian.

May you trust in God for all things, for through Him, nothing is impossible.

I love you.

Alexander hurried into the kitchen, looking for a snack. "I want something good to eat," he said, as he opened the cabinet doors.

"Then it's me you're looking for."

Alexander stopped in his tracks. He was in the kitchen alone.

"Who's talking?" He turned around just as the basket of fruit on the table flipped over.

Out rolled an apple, all shiny and green. "I'm a good for you snack. I'm loaded with fiber and carbohydrates. That means I keep your body strong, help heal your scrapes and wounds, fight off colds and diseases."

A cluster of purple grapes marched forward, "I have vitamins too, plus minerals. I help the body and muscles to be healthy and strong."

Just then a strawberry strutted around, "I'm the one you need for snacking! I'm good for your gums and teeth. I help heal wounds and fight colds. I'm rich in vitamin C. I can help you become stronger!"

The banana split from the bunch declaring, "I should be the number one snacking choice. I have everything Mrs. Strawberry does, plus B vitamins. I help regulate Alexander's heart."

The pineapple roared, "Move over fellows! I'm the **biggest**, the **best**, the **juiciest** fruit here! I'm very nutritious." Then he was rudely interrupted.

Shouting loudly, the orange rolled forward, "*I'm* just as juicy as you, Mr. Pineapple!" Looking around at the other fruit he argued, "*I'm* the best choice. It's easy to see. *I* have calcium for strong teeth and bones. *I* give your skin a healthy glow. *I* fight colds and diseases. *I* regulate your heartbeat. *I* help your muscles and red blood cells. *I* heal sores and make your body stronger!"

A bag of sunflower seeds swiftly cut into Mr. Orange's speech. "You all should be ashamed of yourselves for throwing all this talk at Alex. He is looking for a nutritious snack...that's me! I have a large supply of B-vitamins. My protein gives him more energy."

Smiling sweetly at all the talk going around, Miss Honey Bottle spoke softly, "I'm the snack that's called 'Heaven's Gift.' I've got everything you guys have, yet it only takes a spoonful of me to satisfy. I add that special sweetness to your snacking."

Looking like a satisfied conductor, Alex began to clap. "Great show, guys. My mom told you to do this, right? She's always asking me to eat my fruit."

While shaking their heads no, the fruit, sunflower seeds and honey all looked at Alex.

Mr. Orange looked angry. He yelled loudly at the other fruit, "Get back in the basket! I'm all he needs for snacking."

"Who made you boss?" asked Mrs. Strawberry.

"Yeah, Mrs. Strawberry, you tell him! Grapes are the right choice," shouted Mrs. Grape Cluster, spitting seeds at the others.

Alex fumed, "Stop it...Stop it! I said I wanted a good snack. You know, candy, cake or, maybe, cookies."

The big fellow, Mr. Pineapple, marched right to the edge of the table. He pointed his finger in Alex's face, "Young man, a good snack is not *any* of those things! I'm what your body needs to grow stronger!"

Mr. Apple shook his fist at Mr. Pineapple, "You may be the biggest but remember, I'm packed with more growing power." He pushed Mrs. Banana while shouting at the others, "Split it. Beat it fellows! Back into that basket." He turned around, tripped over Miss Sunflower Seeds and landed on top of Miss Honey Bottle.

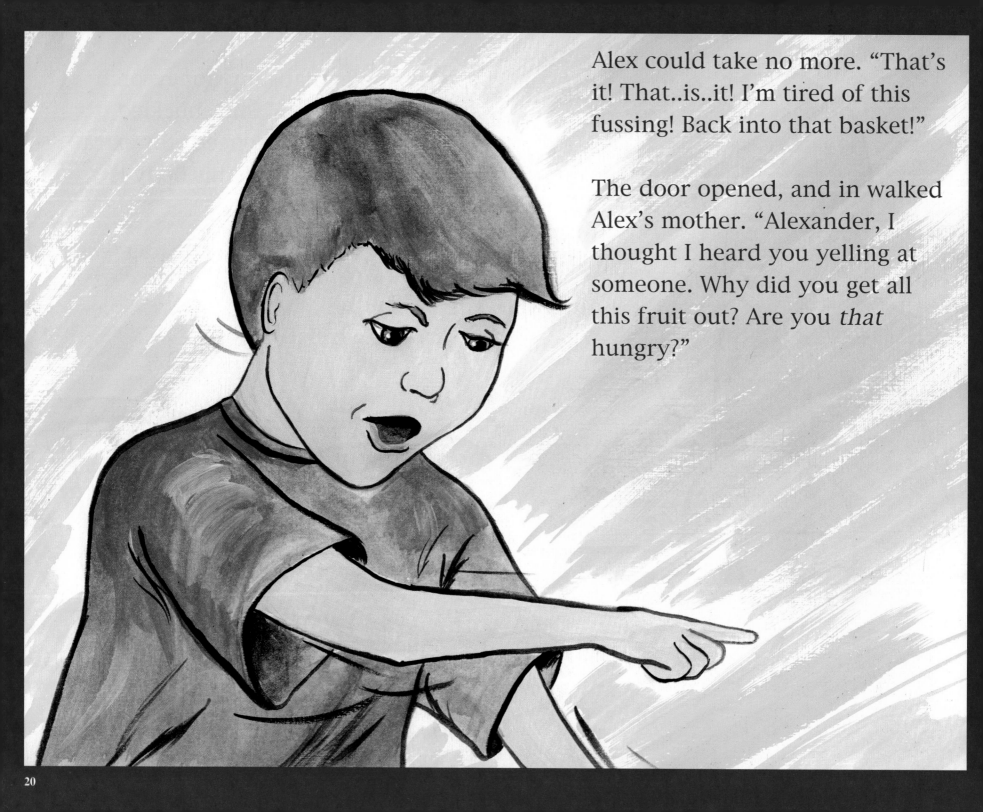

Alex could take no more. "That's it! That..is..it! I'm tired of this fussing! Back into that basket!"

The door opened, and in walked Alex's mother. "Alexander, I thought I heard you yelling at someone. Why did you get all this fruit out? Are you *that* hungry?"

"Uh...I was looking for a snack. I didn't know what to eat. Um...Will you help me make a bowl of fruit salad?"

His mom smiled, "I'm glad you chose a healthy snack instead of sweets."

Alex shyly mumbled, "Fruits help me to grow stronger."

They juiced the pineapple, cut-up the banana, peeled and sliced the orange, chopped the apple, plucked off the grapes, dropped in the strawberries, poured on the honey and stirred, then sprinkled sunflower seeds on top.

As Alex took his last, delicious bite, he sat thinking. "I'm glad the food fight's over and *I'm* the winner."

Nutritional Information

APPLE

The apple is one of the most valuable of all fruits. "An apple a day keeps the doctor away" is no empty saying, because of its value to our bodies. Contains: Fiber, Carbohydrates, Minerals, Protein, Calcium, Phosphorus, Iron, Vitamins A, Vitamin E, Selenium and B-Complex

Nutritional Information

BANANA

The banana is of great food value. It has a rare combination of energy value, tissue building elements, protein, vitamins and minerals. It is richer in solids and lower in water content than any other fresh fruit. Contains: Potassium, Calcium, Phosphorus, Carbohydrates, Vitamin C, Vitamin A, B-complex, Protein, Iron, Selenium and Magnesium

Nutritional Information

GRAPES

The grape is a highly valued fruit mainly for its rich content. Contains: Calcium, Protein, Phosphorus, Minerals, Vitamin C, B-Complex, Vitamin A, Carbohydrates, Iron, Magnesium, and Potassium

Nutritional Information

HONEY

Honey has been considered a perfect food since ancient times. Less than one-hundredth part of it is waste. It's been called a food for the gods. Contains: Most Vitamins, Minerals, Potassium, Copper, Sulphur, Iron, Magnesium, Calcium, Sodium, Silica and Chlorine

Nutritional Information

ORANGE

The orange is a well-flavored citrus fruit, juicy and wholesome. Contains: Vitamin C, Vitamin A, Potassium, Calcium, Carbohydrates, Phosphorus, B-Complex, and Iron

Nutritional Information

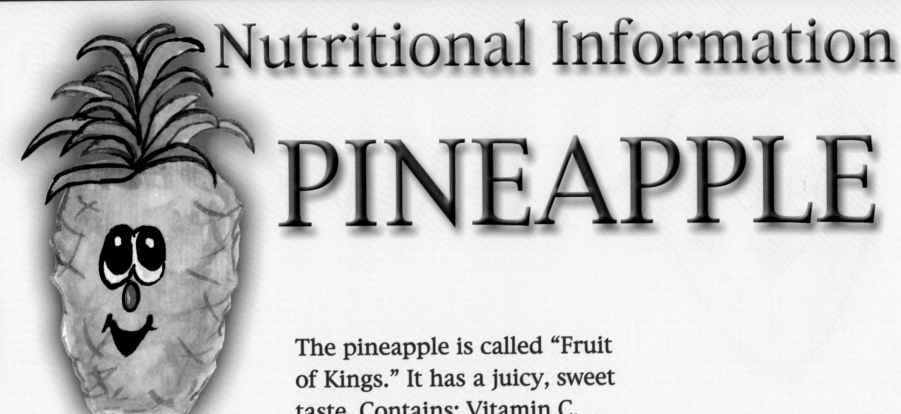

PINEAPPLE

The pineapple is called "Fruit of Kings." It has a juicy, sweet taste. Contains: Vitamin C, Vitamin A, Calcium, Carbohydrates, Potassium, Selenium, Phosphorus, Protein, B-Complex, and Iron

Nutritional Information

STRAWBERRY

The strawberry has a nice bright appearance. Children are drawn to their size for easy handling. Contains: Vitamin C, Carbohydrates, Calcium, Phosphorus, Potassium, Selenium, Vitamin A, B-Complex, Protein, and Iron

Nutritional Information

SUNFLOWER SEEDS

Sunflower seeds can be used as snacks or to enrich any meal. They can be sprinkled over cereals, fruit salads, vegetable salads, yogurts or soup. Contains: B-Complex vitamins, Vitamin E, Selenium, Protein, Carbohydrates, Phosphorus, Calcium and Iron

THE BODY'S USE OF VITAMINS

A: Vital to good vision and important for healthy skin and immunity

B1: Necessary for functioning of brain, nerve cells, and heart

B2: Required to release energy from foods

B3: Maintains healthy skin, nerves, and digestive system

Panto-Thenic Acid: Essential in the synthesis of many body materials

B6: Important in chemical reactions between proteins and amino acids and aids in the formation of red blood cells

B12: Develops red blood cells and maintains the nervous system

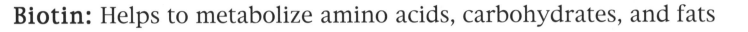

Biotin: Helps to metabolize amino acids, carbohydrates, and fats

Folic Acid: Acts with B12 to produce hemoglobin. It is important in DNA synthesis and prevents neural tube defects (spina bifida).

C: Promotes healthy gums, teeth, and connective tissue. It aids in the healing of wounds. It fights free radicals and strengthens the immune system.

D: Promotes strong bones and teeth and prevents rickets and softening of bones in children

E: Protects tissue against oxidative damage, helps prevent cancer and heart disease

K: Necessary for normal blood clotting

THE BODY'S USE OF MINERALS

Calcium builds healthy bones and teeth. It also regulates blood clotting and prevents muscle spasms.

Copper is necessary for the formation of red blood cells and absorption of iron.

Fluoride contributes to strong bones and teeth.

Iodine maintains normal thyroid function. It prevents goiters and keeps skin, hair and nails healthy.

Iron is very important for the production of blood and muscle functions.

Magnesium is necessary for normal cell function, bone growth, and reproduction.

Potassium regulates muscle contraction and blood pressure. It also controls water balance in tissues and cells.

Phosphorus promotes strong teeth and bones. It is necessary for energy metabolism, and is useful for DNA and RNA synthesis.

Selenium fights cell damage in conjunction with Vitamin E.

Sodium balances water in the body and maintains blood pressure.

Zinc is important for normal growth, fetal growth, reproductive development, and the healing of wounds.

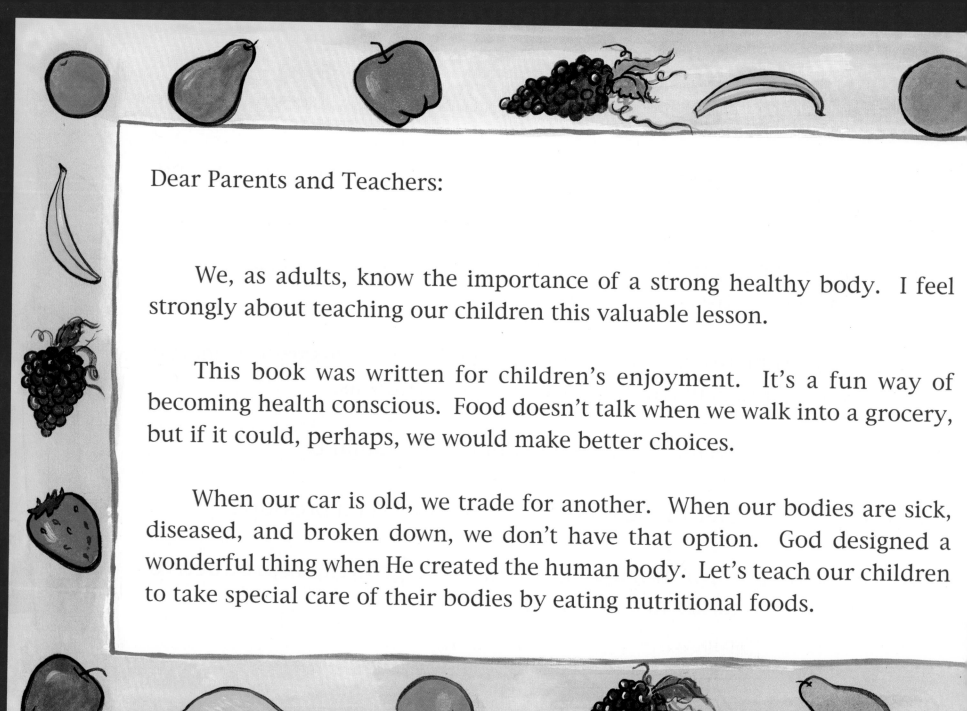

Dear Parents and Teachers:

We, as adults, know the importance of a strong healthy body. I feel strongly about teaching our children this valuable lesson.

This book was written for children's enjoyment. It's a fun way of becoming health conscious. Food doesn't talk when we walk into a grocery, but if it could, perhaps, we would make better choices.

When our car is old, we trade for another. When our bodies are sick, diseased, and broken down, we don't have that option. God designed a wonderful thing when He created the human body. Let's teach our children to take special care of their bodies by eating nutritional foods.

I have found the following to be useful resources for nutritional information:

Eating For Good Health. A *Reader's Digest* Book, produced by Carroll and Browne Limited, London, 1995.

Nine-Day Inner Cleansing and Blood Wash For Renewed Youthfulness and Health. Harold E. Buttram M.D., I.E. Gaumont, 1980.

Food Values Of Portions Commonly Used Thirteenth Edition. Jean A.T. Pennington and Helen Nichols Church, 1980.

I hope that you and your children have enjoyed meeting Alexander and his fruit friends. It has been a pleasure to bring them to you.

Tutti-Fruitti Salad

Items needed:

Large bowl, at least 20-cup size

2-20 oz. cans chunk pineapple (in own juice)

2-15 oz. cans sliced peaches (in own juice)

3 cups yellow apples (approximately 3 or 4 apples)

3 cups red apples (approximately 3 or 4 apples)

3 cups oranges

3 cups purple seedless grapes

2 cups fresh strawberries or 20 maraschino cherries

3 cups sliced bananas

$1/4$ cup of honey

Sunflower seeds or nuts to garnish

12 oz. can diet Sprite (preserves freshness)

*Adult supervision is recommended for preparation of this recipe.

1. Wash all fresh fruit
2. Cut peach slices into smaller chunks (3 or 4 pieces per slice)
3. Pour pineapple, peaches, juices, and diet Sprite into bowl
4. Core apples (do not peel), cut into 1 inch chunks
5. Stir apples in liquid to preserve fruit color and prevent dark coloring
6. Peel oranges, cut into 1 inch chunks
7. Drop in grapes, large ones cut into halves, small grapes leave whole
8. Cap strawberries, cut into halves or quarters
9. Bananas, honey, sunflower seeds, or nuts should be added last before serving. Serve immediately or within a few hours.

*If you plan on refrigerating this salad omit step 9. These ingredients should be added to each bowl before serving. For each individual serving add 1 Tsp. honey, 1/3 sliced banana, top with nuts or sunflower seeds. Honey may be adjusted or omitted according to taste.

Fruit Salad will keep well for 3-4 days in airtight container.